This book belongs to:

The Honey Cake Mix-Up

Disney's Out & About With Pooh
A Grow and Learn Library

Published by Advance Publishers
© 1996 Disney Enterprises, Inc.
Based on the Pooh stories by A. A. Milne © The Pooh Properties Trust.
All rights reserved. Printed in the United States.
No part of this book may be reproduced or copied in any form
without written permission from the copyright owner.

Written by Ann Braybrooks
Illustrated by Arkadia Illustration Ltd.
Designed by Vickey Bolling
Produced by Bumpy Slide Books

ISBN:1-885222-59-9
10 9 8 7 6 5 4 3 2 1

One wonderful morning, when the breeze was scented with new spring blossoms, Winnie the Pooh sat on a log, waiting for Roo.

"I know I promised to help Roo with something today," said Pooh. "I just can't remember what that something is!"

As Pooh licked some honey off his paw, he said, "Now I remember. I promised to help Roo make a honey cake for Kanga's birthday party!"

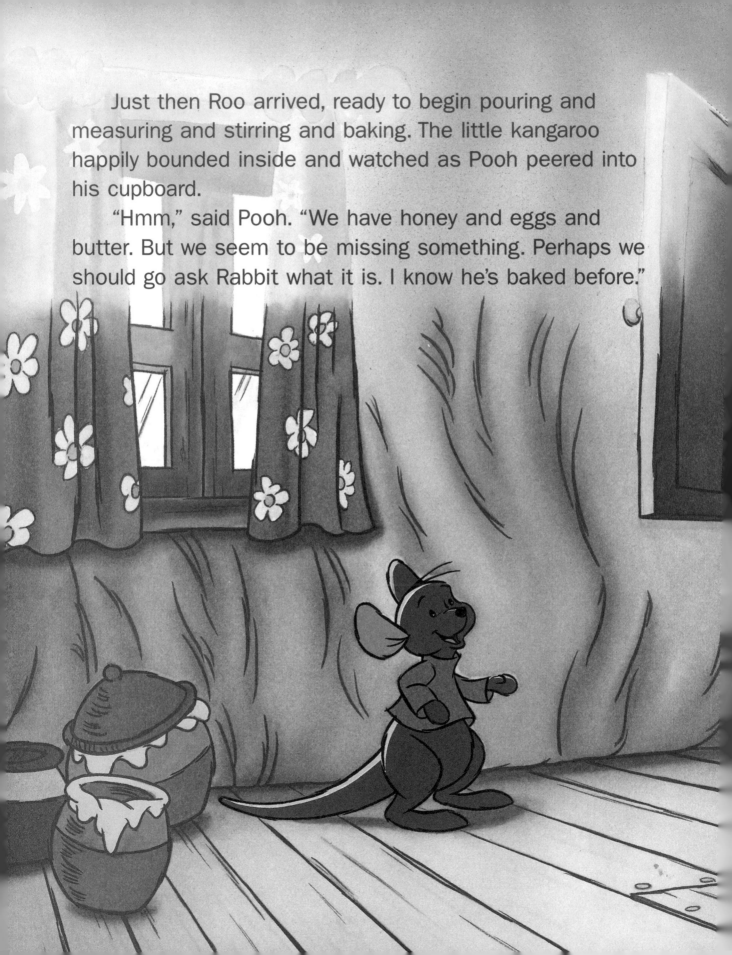

Just then Roo arrived, ready to begin pouring and measuring and stirring and baking. The little kangaroo happily bounded inside and watched as Pooh peered into his cupboard.

"Hmm," said Pooh. "We have honey and eggs and butter. But we seem to be missing something. Perhaps we should go ask Rabbit what it is. I know he's baked before."

"Goodness gracious," said Rabbit, looking in his cookbook. "A honey cake is easy to make! All you need is honey, butter, eggs, baking soda, and flour."

"Ah," said Pooh. "That's what we're missing. The flower."
Pooh was sure that Rabbit meant the kind with petals and
leaves.

"I'd give you the flour," said Rabbit, "but I'm all out."

"That's all right," said Pooh. "Roo and I can find it.
Thank you for your help, Rabbit!"

And so Pooh and Roo strolled into the woods, searching for the perfect flower for Kanga's cake. A little while later, they ran into Piglet.

"We're looking for a flower!" announced Roo excitedly.

"So was I," said Piglet. "And I found a whole bunch of them!" He proudly held out a small bouquet.

"Would you mind showing us where they are?" Pooh asked.

"Not at all," said Piglet. "I'll even help you pick some."

Pooh and Roo picked some flowers then went to Pooh's house. Then they mixed them up with the eggs and butter and baking soda and honey and poured the batter into a cake pan. They put the pan in the oven, anxiously opening the door every few minutes to see if the cake was rising. *It wasn't.*

"Maybe we used the wrong flower," suggested Roo.
"I think you're right," Pooh agreed. And so the two friends
headed out again to find a different flower for Kanga's cake.

It seemed as if they looked at a hundred different flowers. Roo especially liked some tiny yellow ones he saw in the grass.

"Those are buttercups," said Pooh. "We don't want to use those, because we already have a cup of butter at home."

After a while, Pooh and Roo decided to go see Eeyore.

"Oh, good," Eeyore said. "Visitors. Or were you on your way to someplace else?"

"No," said Pooh. "We came to see you. We want to get your advice about something."

"You do?" said Eeyore, surprised that anyone would want to ask his advice about anything. "Such as what?"

"Flowers!" cried Roo.

"Thistles, actually," said Pooh. "How do you think they would taste in a cake?"

"I don't know," said Eeyore. "Why don't you taste some for yourself?"

Eeyore led his friends to a small patch of purple thistles. But when Pooh bent down to pick a flower, he saw that it was covered with prickles.

Pooh said, "Thistles are sort of prickly, don't you think?"

"I suppose," said Eeyore. "But the prickles would give your cake crunch."

Pooh imagined the prickly cake the thistles would make.

Not wanting to hurt Eeyore's feelings, Pooh said, "You know, Eeyore, this is such a lovely patch of thistles that you should have it all to yourself. Roo and I will find another patch. But thank you for all your help."

After they left Eeyore, Pooh and Roo bumped into
Tigger. Or rather, Tigger bounced into them.

"Whatcha doin', Buddy Bear?" Tigger asked Pooh.

"We're looking for the flower to put in Kanga's cake," explained Pooh.

"Do you know where we could find one?" Roo asked hopefully.

"I know where you can find Tigger-lilies," said Tigger.

Pooh said, "You mean tiger lilies. Don't you?"

"Well, some folks call them that," said Tigger, frowning. "But these tiger lilies have *bounce*! Any cake you put them in is sure to rise!"

"What do you think, Roo?" asked Pooh. "Do you want to put a Tigger-lily in your mama's honey cake?"

"Oh, yes!" said Roo, jumping up and down with excitement. "She'll have the highest, bounciest cake ever!"

As soon as Pooh and Roo got home, Pooh mixed the Tigger-lilies with the other ingredients.

Pooh let Roo stir for a while. Then he poured the mixture into a pan.

Before Pooh put the pan in the oven, Roo said, "It looks kind of funny."

Pooh stared at the lumpy orange mixture. "That's because it's not cooked," he said. "It will look different once we bake it."

But when Pooh took the pan out of the oven, nothing had changed.

"Oh, my!" said Pooh. "This doesn't look like a cake at all. It looks like carrot soup!"

Roo peered at the goo. "What did we do wrong?" he asked in a worried voice.

"I think we should go see Rabbit again," said Pooh. "He'll know how to fix it."

Once Rabbit saw the soupy mixture, he said, "Oh, Pooh! You forgot the flour!"

"No, I didn't," said Pooh.

"No, we didn't," echoed Roo.

"Then you mustn't have used the white kind," Rabbit insisted.

"Oh," said Pooh. "I see." But he wasn't quite sure that he did.

"Don't worry, Roo," said Pooh. "We still have a few hours until Kanga's party. We'll find a white flower in no time."

As they were searching, Owl flew overhead.

"Hello, Owl," said Pooh. "Do you know where we could find a white flower?"

"Would a white rose do?" Owl asked. "Christopher Robin has some roses in his garden. He might have a white one."

"That would be splendid!" said Pooh.

"Yes, it would," said Owl, settling on a branch. "By the way, did I ever tell you about my great-aunt Rose? Well, it really is quite fascinating how . . ."

As Owl chattered on, Roo and Pooh slipped away.

A while later, they found Christopher Robin, who had been out back in his garden.

"I was wondering," said Pooh, "do you have a white flower to put in Kanga's cake? We already have the other ingredients."

"Silly old bear," said Christopher Robin. "You need white baking flour, not a white flower with petals and a stem."

"I do?" said Pooh.

"My mother has some in a tin," said the boy. "I'll get it for you."

While Christopher Robin was getting the flour, Pooh and Roo admired the roses. They stuck their noses into the blossoms, breathing in their sweet scent.

"Mmm," said Roo. "They smell like Mama."

Soon Christopher Robin appeared with the tin. As Pooh stared at the white flour inside, Christopher Robin said, "It's okay, Pooh. It's easy to make a mistake, especially with words that sound the same."

"You're right," said Pooh. "Flower and flour. No wonder I got confused."

"You had a good idea, though," said Christopher Robin.
"I'm sure Kanga would love to receive some flowers for her
birthday. Here, why don't you take her these roses? Then
you can give her a bouquet *and* a cake."

That afternoon, Pooh and Roo used the flour
Christopher Robin had given them to make a wonderful, tall,
golden honey cake. When Pooh took the cake out of the
oven, Roo breathed deeply and said, "It sure smells as good
as a flower!"

Later that afternoon, at the party in the woods, Roo gave the honey cake and the bouquet of roses to his mother. "Thank you, Roo," said Kanga. "What wonderful presents these are! And to think that you and Pooh made the cake all by yourselves! Why, you really are quite a pair!"

Pooh began to imagine himself and Roo as big, green pears. He must have looked confused, because Christopher Robin said, "Not that kind of pear, Pooh! Kanga meant the kind of pair that means two!"

Pooh and Roo and Christopher Robin giggled just a little, then sat down to eat big, delicious slices of Kanga's honey cake with their friends.